MW01491590

Elmo Howell

Have you been to Shubuta?

LANGFORD & ASSOCIATES
MEMPHIS

TO HALLIE

Also by Elmo Howell:

MISSISSIPPI HOME-PLACES
WINTER VERSES
MISSISSIPPI SCENES
THE APRICOT TREE
I KNOW A PLANTED FIELD

CONTENTS

I. MORNING

II. NOON

III. THE LONG EVENING

IV. LATE THOUGHTS

ACKNOWLEDGEMENTS

"It is impossible to write the history of Mississippi without writing romance as well."

—Stark Young

Elmo Howell

Have you been to Shubuta?

I

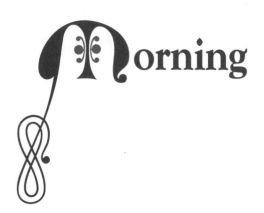

orning

The Battle of Ackia

When the Indians beat the French at Ackia—on
     May 26, 1736, between 2:00 and 5:00 o'clock—
They burnt their prisoners alive at sundown;
Sparing two, to send after Bienville with a
     message:
Come back to see us—they whined—when the
     Chickasaw hogs want slop.
The French never did come back.

I like this soft Prairie knoll,
Lingering in the safety of the rail fence
     about the time of plum blossom.
With echoes of course—all up and down the
     Trace;
A melancholy strain sorting with nature—
Like the song Wordsworth heard.
It's fine to pick up the field lark again—
     nesting, as on the day of carnage.
Even then, no cease of song.

The Burial of DeSoto

Conquistadores

Standing on the courthouse steps, the old
    gentleman dropped a strange coin into
    my hand.
I shuffled it to find, as informed I should,
    the corrugated crest of Castile and León.
He spoke with authority of the Cabildo, the
    Consulate General and of letters patent from
    Madrid.
And of Pieces of Eight!
I held in my hand one Bit—
Turned up by a boy at Losher and West, digging
    a flowerbed for his grandmother—
And recollected ploughed hillsides, with broken
    arrowheads arranged on the window sill by my
    bed;
Though they didn't interest me very much.

The old man's treasure stirred perversely.
Panoply and power amongst us! Monastery walls
    and stalwart men on their knees—
Or just crossing the Tate County line!
With sadness too, for the lost tender of earth—
    and at my foolish predilection.

The Morning They Burned d'Artaguette

Passing this way many years ago, I stopped
　　off to read the marker.
It was on a Sunday morning—and it was on a
　　Sunday morning they burned d'Artaguette.
What secrets of lost woods. What rope's-ends!
They died bravely, records say—seventeen Frenchmen,
　　moving decorously into the fire prepared for
　　them—
The priest in front, intoning the Miserere;
But a young monk clutched at Father Senac's side.
We all are not born to this.

These were not our people.
Both victim and victor, those who were consumed
　　and those who watched,
Have gone from the land, or left charred bones
　　to reckon with.
Their passage is like a dream.
Other men came and set up the marker.

The Royal Touch

Let there be ceremony! the British said—degree,
   priority and place.
But it was tough going in the wilderness—
A brother to King George, his squaw squatting
   behind him.
General Jackson was not so nice; and after a brief
   reign, King Ishtehotopah packed up and left—
A royal throne in King's Creek Bottom—but
   something more wonderful than that—
Something to outlast state.

> Old Mohataha, Queen of the Chickasaws, led
>   her people out of the land.
> Sprawled in a wagon beneath a French parasol
>   held by the negro slave girl,
> She rode into Jefferson for the last time—
>   out of the woods into the dusty clearing
>   in front of Ratcliffe's store—
> To set her capital X.
> Where IS this Indian Territory? she said.
> They told her, West.
> Turn the wagons west, she said.
> And they did—
> Vanishing across that summer afternoon in the
>   creak and creep of ungreased wheels—
> Riding off the stage under the tilting parasol,
> Sculpted, imperial; bizarre and moribund:
> Looking not back, not once back towards home.

That's pretty good.
And that's what it came down to—
A marker on Highway 15 and one long line in a
   book.

On The Leaf River Bridge At McLain

When the land belonged to Spain,
Dark men came up Leaf one night heavy with
    gold—and shipped out at dawn, light
    as sea turtles.
Farmers found it, stopped ploughing and
    went to the house—
And mean men came in the night with shovels.

One afternoon at City Hall I asked an old
    gentleman about it.
"I've got a piece," he said.
"You have?" I said. "Could I just have a
    look?"
"You can't," he said. "It's in my box in
    Hattiesburg."
A lady said an old black man had one bigger
    than a dollar.
"Bright as my wedding ring," she said, and
    showed me her band.
"Lester," she said, "somebody will knock you
    in the head for that."
But they didn't.
He carried it in his pocket till the day
    he died.

And old Leaf River rolls on.
Ghosts on the perilous bend!
I don't walk out very far, I wait here by
    my car in the smell of snake and watermelon
    in West Florida.
Off and away to the Chickasawhay,
Down the Pascagoula singing.

The Mexican's Grave

West of Thomastown, the old Pickens Road
    fades out in a timber farm.
Kirkwood was never a town, nor in the true
    sense a village.
It was a jewel set on a hill.
Great people came with chattel and their
    heads up to play at life there;
Stakes were high—
And I got out of my car in the desolation of
    scrub pine.
Not one brick marks a house or a garden
    wall.
Only Governor McWillie's tall monument stands
    up in the undergrowth (not far I believe
    from St. Philip's and the rectory);
And in the shadow of that lonely insistence,
    I found the Mexican's grave.
His slab was broke and lay on it.

GREGORIS CERVANTES
Born in
GUADALAXARA
MEXICO
Died October 23, 1852
Aged
About 25 Years

Old writers speak of the speciality of Kirkwood.
In 1850, Jefferson Davis and Senator Toombs of
    Georgia came to a great dinner.

General

General Quitman came—Governor Mathews, Governor
    Foote, Governor Pettus, Governor McRae.
And Bishop Green of course.
But who was this interloper—the dark stranger
    so honored in death?
A visiting minister of state? A protocol?
Or only a favorite slave?
I think it must have been that—some vagary of
    the heart.
Earth's grief betraying delight—
In a lost fiefdom where nobody comes anymore.

The House In Wayne County

William Powe went first, with a lightwood knot at
  his head,
Behind the house where he smoked the peace pipe with
  his neighbors.
Then Elizabeth Pegues Powe, his wife.
They established this plantation on a Georgia land grant,
And after the peace of many wars, still wait a
  ratification—
And for us to call on an April afternoon.

We drove slow, in state, through cow dung
(The key to the drive was hid in a stump);
Crawled through fences, like children, onto a buttercup
  lawn where old trunks sprouted a little—
And walked right up to our house.
And to so much more.
Through barred windows, a grizzled black man poked dead
  coals, wide-eyed—he didn't see us—
With guns in place on the third floor!
It was the dreadful summer of Fort Mims.

> On August 29, 1813, two Negroes minding beef
> cattle rushed into the Fort with word of war-painted
> Indians—and were whipped for false alarm. At noon
> the following day, when the drum sounded for dinner,
> 1000 Creek sprung the camp as one man—the East Gate
> could not be closed, sand having washed against it.
>
> After four hours of carnage, the survivors collected
> in the "Bastion," an old loom house with some extra
> picketing, to form one immense mass of human beings too
> close to defend themselves—waiting in a pen like
> beeves for the butcher. "All were scalped, and the

females

females of every age were butchered in a manner which neither decency nor language will permit me to describe."

The population of Fort Mims was more than 500. Only about a score escaped, among them a Mrs. McGirth, a half-breed, and her seven children; Socca, a friendly Indian; and the Negro slave Hester, who, though wounded in the breast, reached a canoe in the lake and took word to General Claiborne at Fort Stoddard.

I wandered into a hayfield for a perspective of sun—on gray
    gables, like New England.
How many today have seen this place? You can't see it from
    the road.
But what is there to see?
And who is there to listen? To take on the probability of
    Indians, lost wars, and a gate that couldn't be closed?
(Was Claiborne correct in repeating these things?)
I don't think the old house meant to hang on so long.

I Shall Not Read
The Footnotes Of Claiborne

I shall not read the footnotes of Claiborne,
    nor much of the fine print—
Saving something for the next time.
I never read straight through nor look for
    the big picture—
But farm out a passage here and there and make
    notes in the margin.
What a moon-landing event Claiborne is! At
    least by the old reckoning.
Though a patriot and certainly our premier
    historian, life must go on, he seems to say—
And pulls aside to enjoy it:
Lambaste, declaim a little or tend a gossip.

> Judge Powhatan Ellis, with his
> Pocahontas blood, was the most indolent
> man in the Territory. "Though an inveterate
> smoker, he has often been known to take his
> seat by the fire and sit for two hours with
> a cigar in his mouth, until a servant passing
> by would hand him a coal to light it."

If you think this is trash, I'm sorry.
Claiborne gets beside himself—he's better
    than Faulkner.
Gibbon too had fun with history.

Hinda and Hafed

Hinda's Bower

General Reuben Davis was set like a rock—
But his wife was a zephyr (his first one I mean),
    a song, a mist from the mountain where the
    peries fix their abode.
She was barren, poor lady, so took to the
    imagination, which has been the undoing of
    many good people.
He built her Suristan. (Cypress still grieve—
    west of the river, just off the bypass.)
He built her follies and the moated isle, where
    she did sit and dream of love—
More feminine than herself the perfumed head
    of Hafed!—
And dress her poem for the next day's post.

If you go to the Evans Memorial Library in Aberdeen,
To the high shallow shelves for a DEMOCRAT or
    SUNNY SOUTH, which will take a little doing,
You can see for yourself: the lady Hinda, leaning
    from a bower with LALLA ROOKH—
In a raw land that does not know the name.
Her husband wrote too and was much admired,
    but loved Hinda first.
Did she love him?
Of course she did.
"We were happy as the birds." he said, "and had
    almost as little care for the future."

The Purnells of Montgomery County

The hill proclaimed gables, with maple and
    sassafras brushing the upstairs windows.
A doe startled at the gate, making up her mind
    which way to go. We waited for her.
Blackberries were coming in in the front yard.
Thomas Purnell and his wife Eunice settled
    here in the 40's, built this house and
    died young—
That's about all we know.
The house has little history, little report—the
    historical society hasn't wet its shoes.
But chimneys knew Christmases,
The makings of an old road brought up news.
And the hunter still stomps by a notice in the
    woods.

> This monument marks the center of a
> square four-acre parcel of land on the
> plantation of Micajah Thomas Purnell, set
> apart by him in the year 1844, as a burying
> ground for his family and slaves; whose
> descendants shall have the right to bury
> free of charge here forever.

They came out of the east in wagon trains,
Positioned, like the doe, for Maytime and an
    occasion of weather.
Then the coach pulled around.
The gallery was a bustle of farewell and
    not forgetting—
And somebody pulled the door to.

Governor Joseph W. Mathews

Looking For Governor Mathews's Grave

The stout-hearted lady from Tippah led out—
    "We're off, Governor! We're on our way"—
And leaving the car at a white man's house
    (It's over in the woods, they said, but it
    wasn't),
Overtook an old man trying to jog.
He was going that way, if we'd just tag along.
A woman came out on the porch to wave—her dog
    joined in, his tongue out too.
At a colored man's house the old man stopped—
    for a time-of-day. The little boy knew the
    stout-hearted lady and came along too to do
    what he could.
"We're coming, Governor!
But, Governor, where are you hiding?"
Over in old Marshall was all we knew.
The world made way—they knew our need;
For Excellency was waiting, the Head of State!
By a pediment of laurel, under an old magnolia
    tree:
With something to say on the Wilmot Proviso;
Or the Compromise of 1850 on which there could
    be no compromise.
Old Joe Salem! Old Copperas Britches! The
    one with the fist in his face.
When he stood up, other men sat down.
"We're with you, Governor. We're coming!"

The Cholera Year

Governor Abram Scott, our fifth governor,
  was in excellent health all afternoon—
But what is this life of man? says Job.
A young man with an exemplary record on
  the Territorial staff,
Governor Scott punished the Indians,
  collected the taxes and came before
  his time to honors of state.
He was a Whig (before Jackson's men came
  down) and set store on the moment—
How a man lives and how he dies;
And died that night like any black slave!
At the home of his friend Colonel Grimball,
  where he'd stopped off to make a call.

The Hanging Tree

The jail in Athens is 150 years old:
   "walls brick-over-logs 32" thick; beams
   between floors 12" square; windows
   double-hung, nine over six."
The oak tree in front was the hanging tree.
When the courthouse burned, they held court
   under it—and led the poor devil back
   upstairs to look out the window a few days—
And have conversation with the tree.
They left a lot to the tree.
It spoke plain to him and waited for an
      answer;
So that at last he saw what he was.

Athens is gone.
The court changed venue. Law-abiding citizens
   moved out with the various churches and the
   Temperance Society.
They hauled down the flag and filled in the well.
But the jail is still there—
And the ghost of a tree still holds up to empty
   windows that antique assessment.
The rest picked up in Aberdeen.

II

Noon

Quitman At Monmouth

New England came South grimacing, bought slaves,
    and ran the country.
Governor Sargent became a great Mississippian—
    and it didn't matter that Prentiss left his heart
    in Maine.
But Quitman was Quitman only at Monmouth.
He remembered the old apple tree too of course,
    as the novice remembers—and picked up from there.
His life was a beautiful harmony, says Claiborne.

When. Mrs. General Claiborne asked him to dine—
    or Dr. Dunbar or Judge Turner—
The young man from New York was eager to oblige;
And in the long evenings at Propinquity, the Forest
    or Soldier's Retreat,
He fell on a fiction—an ideality—that fashioned
    his life.

> "Cordial hospitality is a characteristic of these
> people," he wrote home. "Their very servants catch
> the feeling and anticipate one's wants: your coffee
> in the morning before sunrise; little stews and
> sudorifics at night, and foot-baths if you have a
> cold; bouquets of flowers and a mint julep sent
> to your apartment; a horse and saddle at your
> disposal. I seem to be leading a charmed life here."

War came—and the South looked up.
General Quitman crossed the plains and the desert
    mountains.

                                                He

He took Monterrey, the fortified cities, and stood
    up at Belen Gate.
He stood where Cortez stood—" O war, thou hast thy
    fierce delights!"—
And still looked out!
The brigand race subdued, a continent waited, curving
    south—
The Yucatan, Middle America—an empery of the Southern
    seas!
In those headlong days, men thought like that.

Out of the affections, Quitman took vows.
At Monmouth he hoed in his garden in the morning and
    trimmed his vines.
Ambassadors stopped off to call.
He was not a man of intellect, says Claiborne.
His strength was in his face and in the breast of a
    young man—
Caught up in the destiny of a really fine people,
    sauntering in a garden on a summer afternoon.

The Flag

Sovereignty waits on a flag—but nobody thought
    about that;
Except one lady.
On January 9, 1861, Hurrah and Still Faces were
    having it out. Hurrah was everywhere.
In the middle of the morning, one Mrs. Smythe took
    off to her dressmaker's.
"We need a flag, Mrs. Dudley. We need it this
    morning!"
Mrs. Dudley summoned a helper, Miss Em Sue Cadwallader
    from Lockport, New York, who set straight to work.
At the crux of noon, a lady mounted the Capitol steps.
She saluted a friend, Mr. C. D. Dickson, who bore
    her favor to the President of the Convention, the
    Hon. William S. Barry of Lowndes County.
The moment was right.
And whatever went through the President's mind, he
    unfurled a silk flag,
A flag that bore a single star.
The chamber hushed—the crowd said Yes;
And word was borne down Capitol Street, north and
    south on State—
Sweeping over the city to the boom of cannon on the
    river.
The die was cast—and the telegraph sent wires to
    thirteen states.

But whoever heard of that day now? Or the bonnie blue
    flag they stood to?
Or of the gallant lady who brought it?
                            She

She was the wife of Homer Smythe, printer; and daughter
  of Marcus Hilzheim, a merchant of Jackson—that's
  all I know.
Or of Miss Cadwallader of upstate New York?
Surely she deserves a little credit too.

The Battle Of Rodney

After Vicksburg, Yankees lay fat about the land.
At Rodney, across from the Presbyterian Church, the
gunboat "Rattler," U.S.A., kept watch on the town,
its crew swaggering in the streets.
The Captain had heard of their buttermilk cavalry,
he told the locals one day. First Officer Ensign
Strunk was with him—and they would be over some
morning to whip them with cornstalks.
On the bluff above the church, Lt. Cicero Allen and
his 15 men, C.S.A., were in bivouac.
It was Saturday evening at mess, when a carriage drew
up and a lady summoned the young lieutenant to her
side.
She told him about the Captain and Ensign Strunk and
what the Captain said. She told him about the
cornstalks.
The Lieutenant bowed, thanked the lady, and returned
to his supper.
On Sunday morning—September 13, 1863—just at the
beginning of the second hymn,
An officer in gray walked up the aisle and whispered
in the minister's ear.
The organ stopped. He turned to the congregation—
and told 22 Yankees what to do;
A bullet grazed the Lieutenant's face—and war broke
out.
The congregation dove—but one old lady shouted from
her pew—she climbed up on it! Glory to God!
Glory to God!

The

The "Rattler" heard and laid down fire—you can see it
    on the church today.
With a Captain by the heels and 15 men laid out behind
    him, Lt. Allen issued an order—
He tore a leaf from his notebook and wrote it:
"Stop firing on Rodney, or I'll hang every man in my
    possession."
The order was transmitted, the firing ceased,

And that was the Battle of Rodney—not heard around
    the world but in the breast of a little town starved
    for victory.
The "Rattler," still watching, looked silly;
The Captain and Mr. Strunk filed their report from Libby
    Prison in Richmond.
They were treated bad, they said.
They were tied to a horse and made to keep pace for more
    than five miles, they said.
Lt. Allen got them out of there.

Every Courthouse Needs
A Monument

'Tis not in mortals to command
success; but we'll do more,
Sempronius. We'll deserve it,

Crossing the square in the tumult of morning
    and the work ethic (It was not in my state),
I marveled at quietness—
Which came over the city from deliberate
    stone and the peace of old books.
Every courthouse needs a monument.
And today when I come to an empty square—I
    look on all sides!—
I feel left off in an unfinished country.
A monument is not to read, really, or look
        up to—but to walk past on the way to the
        bank or to pay taxes and throw up your hand
        to somebody.
Isn't that the way we know one another?
Surely some little greatness could be remembered.

Ship Island. Sep.t

My darling little boys and little Emma

As I cannot write separately to
each of you — and I am very anxious
to reply to my dear Randolphs very
excellent and well written letter — and
also to Emma whose letter was
very nice — you must all be sat-
-isfied with this and believe that
Dear Mother never allows a day
to pass without thinking of all
her loved little ones, and a night
to arrive without praying to God
to keep you all well and make
good, obedient children of you all.
My darling Randy, I have no doubt
you are a good little boy and do all
your dear sister Fan wishes you
to do, for she writes me word that
she is pleased with your conduct
and this makes Mother very happy

42

A Confederate Woman's Journal

When Beast Butler sat in New Orleans, hauling in ladies
   for humming a tune,
Mrs. Eugenia Levy Phillips was amused—and laughed
   injudiciously one day.
The old Puritan growled:
And on June 30, 1862—in accordance with Special Order
   No. 150—Eugenia Levy Phillips, "a vociferous Rebel,"
   was consigned to Ship Island.
Which was a sink.
A phantasmagoria of soldiers, sailors, officers,
   contractors, butlers, sutlers, peddlers, Black
   Republicans, snakes and mosquitoes, and Negro devotees
   who moaned all night.
Being a lady, the prisoner was tendered a boxcar, where
   she and her maid Phebe sat under an umbrella till the
   shower passed;
And ate Yankee food.
She spoke to the Sergeant—the Captain, the Major.
She summoned Colonel Dow.
She told them with her tongue, and she told them with
   the way she stood in the door—
Retiring it would seem to siesta—or perhaps to her
   reticule for French, her Journal, or THE VICAR OF
   WAKEFIELD.
"Ah, the dear Vicar. This morning I had another chat
   with my dear old friend the Vicar."
And what can you do with a woman like that?
In late September, having agreed with the Provost
   Marshall that she was indeed "an enemy of the United
   States" (as General Butler said),
                                                    She

She waved farewell to the boxcar and sailed to the arms
of her husband and five small children.
And to the gratulation of a city—who called but
didn't know what to say.
Mrs. Eugenia Levy Phillips!
Old men came out and stood bareheaded before her.

Why Giles Plantation Is Still Laughing

When she heard the Yankees were coming, burning
    everything high and low,
Old Mrs. Jacob Giles got ready.
When the Captain dismounted at the foot of the
    drive, a servant went out with a silver tray—
And on it lay the key to the house!
The mistress waited at the door—
The tour began.
First, the east parlor—under the acanthus leaf
    rosette:
"Does I hit him now, Mistis?"—old Tom at her
    elbow, his walking stick up.
"No, Tom. Not yet."
The Captain took his time.
The steeplechase was on. Around the house through
    the scuppernong frame! There goes the lot gate!
    With every hen off her nest.
The wide-eyed door jambs didn't move a muscle.
He turned to the stairs, the long empty ballroom—
    positioning by the window to hear the place roar,
The lady with a lamp stood by his side.
Then slowly, slowly, past the dark corner by Mrs.
    Murphy's room—
"Does I hit him now, Mistis?"
"No, Tom. Not now."
It was really a bed-and-breakfast affair—till the
    Yankee mind made up.
He would take the Empire bed. That would
    do very well.

                               (In

(In the Chamber called Peace that openeth on the
      sunrising!)
And something clicked in the old woman's throat,
      like a clock before it strikes.
Tom, you rascal. Lay down your stick.

And that's why Giles Plantation is still laughing.—
      on the left, Highway 16, just short of Alabama.
All dressed up to go somewhere.
But it looks that way every morning.

At The Beauvoir Ticket Office

What a beautiful view!
That's what a lady said once, and I think so too—
    walking across from the parking lot to the
    hospital.
It was built as a hospital actually,
For old soldiers, sailors, their widows, orphans
    and slaves;
Hustled here at the world's end to wait.
For the time comes when the island no longer
    enchants,
When there's nothing in the south wind nor in
    the jasmine by the door jamb to hurt.
Beyond the East Cottage, the great hollow house
    awaits guests,
With frescoed ceiling and a lost music book.
Accusing, trying to lay blame.
Why here the proffered hand?
Here where the melody has not quite played out—
    and tilt of head that cannot be unlearned.
The mime.
An old black woman breaks through to catch
    what was said.
What's that? The last boat out!
Wouldn't miss it.
We're going this 'n together.

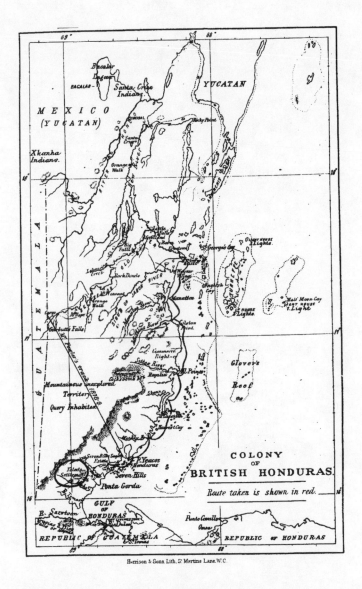

COLONY
OF
BRITISH HONDURAS.

Route taken is shown in red.

The Exiles

They fled Culloden with a claymore—and a tartan
    they wore by day and slept under at night.
It was the same in the Revolution, at the Widow
    Moore's Bridge.
It was always the same with the Scots and Scots-Irish—
    digging in for a stand, with an eye to the west:
For every Appomattox is where you start from.
When the time came, Governor McRae knew what to do.
His people came to Wayne County and dispossessed the
    Indians.
They built Philadelphus Church, cleared the forest
    and dredged the streams—
Their craft made way to Enterprise—
And John J. McRae governed the state.
He sat in the assembly of the new nation at Richmond—
But where is home?

> "Toledo Settlement was established by settlers
> from the Southern States of America. On comfort-
> able homesteads, they grow chiefly sugarcane
> and manufacture the produce into common moscovado
> sugar in open pans. The quality of the sugar is
> of a superior kind.
> "It is to be hoped that they will in time turn
> their attention to other and equally productive
> industries, such as cacao, nutmeg, oranges, lemons,
> bananas, coco-nuts, ginger, Sarsaparilla, arrowroot,
> vanilla, black pepper, which can be grown as easily
> and with as much certainty of a good market.
> "Among the settlers who have established them-
> selves here are Mr. Wilson at Refuge; the Messrs.
> Perrot and Paine at Mount Hope; Messrs. Hutchinson

and

and Been at Mount Royal; Mr. Waterous and son at
Forest House; and Mr. Pearce at Forest Cottage.
    "This is one of the most southerly settlements
in British Honduras, about 20 miles from the Sarstoon
River and the Republic of Guatemala."

In January 1868, a new contingent of 113 Southern people
    sailed from New Orleans to British Honduras.
Governor McRae and his sister were among them.
It was the cholera year.
On May 31, the Governor died—at the home of his
    brother Colin McRae of the Toledo Settlement.
I do not know if his grave has a marker.

Two Flags

The old man was waiting in the porch swing.
It was a hundred years after the war, but two
    flags flew over his post office—
And he wanted to show me.
I'd heard the story—told in pride but also
    with alarm.
When will they come! his neighbors asked. Surely the
    Government men will come.
But he was old, just looking for a fight;
Hoisting his flag in the morning, hoping that
    it mattered and that somebody would look up
    in earnest.

Long after the Forty-Five, an ageing Prince
    came back to a secret shore.
Highlanders flocked to him, the flower of the
    Western shires—looking over their shoulders.
At last the Duke's men came—dry spies—to
    smile on the poor remnant.
We do not know this man, they said to the empty
    hills.
We do not know, we do not care.
Then, Sir, said Redgauntlet—the Cause is lost
    forever!

St. John's Church

The Ruins of St. John's

"For the celebration of Episcopal rites and
    for no other purpose whatsoever..."
So said Jonathan McCaleb of Greenfield Plantation.
The Wade Hamptons were in it, two generations;
    the Turnbulls, Chapmans, Duncans, Butts,
    Hamills,
And one stout-hearted lady, Gracia Turnbull Walton,
    who rode horseback across the country to pledge
    a melodeon from England—
And played it herself the day the bishop came.
The sexton, a Turnbull slave, had charge of the
    woodwork—
And Jesse Crowell's leaf design bloomed for the
    Bishop!
(When Jesse died, Bishop Green came back to the
    parish.)
The church is gone now, just what you see; the
    glebe farmed out to other purposes.
Children play in the ruins—
And one day a certain black boy looked up to the
    great window wreathed in cow's itch—
He grew up to write a book, ONCE UPON A TIME, and
    became a famous man.

> When Miss Shugg's house caught fire,
> They all turned up in the bucket brigade,
>   black and white together.
> Some ran in—dared—to save Miss Shugg's
>   things. And her puppies!
> Her house was infested with puppies.
> They saved every one!

                                                             But

But not the house.
Then the bucket brigade broke up, speaking
       words of sorrow.
Going again their separate ways.

I like St. John's Church.
On All Souls Day, they come back with their priest,
       to intone among ruins the providence of time;
       not seeing the foulness in the rose window.
Children still play on summer afternoons.
They don't know what they see, but have something
       to look up to.

The Old Slave House

The house was a mystery.
I'd read old reports, but nobody knew anything—
    at least they didn't tell me.
It was very grand, they said. The bell was cast
    from 600 silver dollars, and 600 hands took off
    to the fields. Or was it a thousand?
Out towards Alabama, off 510.
The Prairie was sad, empty of mules—but beautiful
    with patches of plum trees.
I stopped off by a black man mowing his yard.
"You mean the old slave house?" he said.
I'd never heard a house called that before.
"Yes," I said. "I think that's it."
And it was. Grander than Natchez, appropriating a
    whole hill in the dignity of park and outbuildings.
But empty, like the land.
I felt left out. There was no one to talk to—
And standing at the gate to take my
    picture (I spotted the old jail, it was round
    like a lighthouse),
I asked myself, What are you doing here?
This is not your business.
How can you hope to know this house?
How can the professor know who will come some day
    and write a report?
Perhaps we've thought too much on these things.

On the way back I stopped off again by the black man's
    house;
But he'd finished mowing and his pickup was gone.

The Beeches Of Union County

Men die—but beech trees live forever.
Knox Wilkins favored the beech, fair and smooth
    to the touch.
He came back from the war and found the old
    folks alone in the house.
Nimrod came back too.
But the young ones didn't come back.

    Jonathan N. went first, in a Richmond hospital
        in '62.
    Five months later, James Clark lay at Corinth
        three days wanting to come home.
    William J. in '64, killed on picket near
        Atlanta.
    Oregon T. in an Illinois prison, just before
        the end.

Nim made a garden, cooked, and brought the medicine
    glass;
Knox mastered the land, which changes as men die
    but stays on.
Out of the gelded hills, the brothers became rich
    and fat.
They paid more taxes than anybody in Union County
    and when they died left gold upstairs—
And hanging from a beam in order of death,
    four suits of clothes.
And that was that—
Except on the great wounded beeches in King's Creek
    bottom.
Every so often the time came, and Knox went out to
    another tree.

The Lost Graves

In the wooded hillcountry above Tupelo,
   just off the Trace,
U.S. officials have set markers to thirteen
   graves.
They make no bones about it, they don't know
   who they are—
But offer an old wives' tale or two:
Forrest's men caught in an ambush;
General Lee's rear guard in redeployment after
   Harrisburg;
Or poor stragglers from Corinth, beaten and
   lost—who found somebody here to die
   with.
Lined up by a road where no wheel turns and
   no wayfarer pauses to read.

I have been to Shiloh and Vicksburg and stood
   before the great monuments;
I've read noble sentiments—and turned away,
   not knowing how to feel.
Here in these woods there is no problem.
It's like coming home;
After so many years coming home too late—
Finding myself left to say the last word.

The Pride of St. Lazarus

While a certain rich man fared
sumptuously every day, clothed in
purple and fine linen, a beggar lay
at his gate full of sores;
and dogs did come to lick…

When Sherman marched in and pressed the city,
      not least the church,
The Rev. Dr. George W. White at Calvary got
      wind that horses would soon feed from
      his pews.
He forwith took the oath—
And Calvary continued to feed the sheep.

The beaten men came home—to the new shepherds
      binding up wounds—
And built St. Lazarus, on Madison between
      Third and Fourth.
Jefferson Davis, of the Carolina Life Insurance
      Company, went to St. Lazarus.
They all went there!
It stood in the city, a brand from the burning,
      till the Yellow Fever year—and the poor
      remnant fled to Grace, at Vance and Lauderdale.
And the Library told me they never heard of St.
      Lazarus.
That side of Madison is a parking lot now,
      with a Blood Bank and the Memphis Day Care Center.
Just two blocks up, Calvary waxes old, richest
      of the diocese.
Dr. White's name is written in the book.

III

The Long Evening

Have You Been To Shubuta?

Don't bring me a Cook's or your old $5.00-a-Day.
The barefoot regimen is over.
What business have I with Old Masters, and bundling
    from the station at midnight with no place to
    lay my head?
Don't make me remember.

But give me a fair morning and the road winding down
    to a country I know—
Tchula, Toomsuba, Shubuta, Shuqualak;
Little towns lost in the crease of my map.
I shall be welcome, at whatever time of arrival,
In the company of intimate strangers—and a
    ritual of dead voices in which I find my
    voice too.
If I stop over, I shall know the virtue of sleep—
And what I will have for breakfast; and what the
    waitress will say as she lingers at my table
    with the coffee pot.
Have you been to Shubuta?
Let us drive down and see what's going on there.
It's on the Chickasawhay.

Pond Store

I like to happen up on old places.
At first it was "the pond," for ox and mule
    on the way to Fort Adams.
Then the Jews came to run a store—and the
    post office said "Pond."
Jews and more Jews, most of them German:
Lehman, Samuel and Lowenburg, the Aaron
    Mercantile Co., Bessie Mount, Ellis T. Hart,
    Morris H. Rothchild, and a Russian, Julius
    Lemkowitz—
Who traded off to a Christian in 1933—and that
    was the end of the line.
And almost the end of the store.
(Jews were everywhere once in the backcountry—
    even in Wahalak on the Alabama line.
    If you don't believe me, go read the
    monument in DeKalb.)
But Carroll Smith and his people held on—
With the old showcases, cash register, the post
    office safe (which belonged to Mr. Mount), a
    cheese cutter, tobacco cutter, lanterns, scales,
    wooden crates, and a cracker box with a Polly
    Parrot on it—
Dozing off in the afternoon with the doors open.
The donkeys I believe were for somnolence—and a
    flock of guineas on the hillside.
(The pond has withdrawn to a pair of gray geese.)
I was on my way to Pinckneyville and stopped off
    for directions.

Judge Kimbrough's
House In Greenwood

"**B**e careful, my dear," old Mrs. Jefferson Davis
    told her.
"When our women marry, they're like Sterne's
    starling—they can't get out."
Mary Craig understood all this. She married a
    Socialist and never looked back;
Though she did miss the big house in summer, the
    grounds sprawling down to the Yazoo—
Her people everywhere.
Upton never liked the South. But that was all right.
She liked to reconcile and to be reconciled—and
    carried a placard too when the time came , even
    invading Mr. Rockefeller's private property.
She scrimped and saved, cooked and patched for
    the starry-eyed line:
Listening, hoping, trying to believe—even having
    a little fun.
Poor Upton!

> Far away in the afternoon, scuppernong
> grapes were swelling on the vine and turning
> brown and would soon be sweet and ripe. So
> would the figs on the Judge's enormous tree.
> Wagons filled with watermelons were stopping
> at the gate. She would send Walter that yellow
> boy out to thump and find ripe ones. It was
> Utopia in her world again.

If you want to see Judge Kimbrough's house today,
    go out Money Road to just across the Tallahatchie
    bridge.
                                                 It's

It's there on the right, in the middle of a cottonfield.
Mary Craig would have gone along too the day they rolled
   it off—taking on a new beat as best she could;
And old Mrs. Davis wouldn't have said a word.

The House At Friars Point

The old river towns went under long ago:
Grand Gulf, Greenville, Commerce Landing, Delta,
    Prentiss, Napoleon.
Now the river keeps mostly to itself—
But at Friars Point comes right up to
    Mr. Marinelli's door!
His yard backs up to the levee.
I got out of my car and listened—but
    couldn't hear a thing. You wouldn't
    know it was there.
If I wanted to see it, he said, I could
    take the ramp to the limestone factory—
And there it was! Flat, immediate—all
    that movement and no sound!
In the war, they lodged a minié ball in
    the house. Mr. Marinelli showed me.
Then a Yankee general lived in it.
More floods came, and they pulled the house
    back to build the levee,
So that now it's on Second Street.
In the library, a romantical fellow thought
    the town was named for DeSoto's crew.
I liked that.
But Robert Friar was the first man to settle
    there.
He was the first to take on that silence.

G. A.
SON OF S. E.
&
J. E. WHITE.
BORN A. D. 1867,
KILLED IN
CYCLONE,
IN BEAUREGARD,
APRIL 22, A. D.
1883.
A GOOD BOY TAKEN AWAY
SUDDENLY AND I BELIEVE
IN HEAVEN

The Day Beauregard Blew Away

On April 22, 1883, the little town bustled on
    the railroad:
On April 23, the Memphis APPEAL ran a headline:
    "Beauregard Mississippi No Longer Exists!"
Mrs. L. A. Hines stood on her front gallery that
    Sunday afternoon.
The southwest—gathering—collected on a track and
    headed like a black train straight into town.
She was there in the aftermath, picking up, laying
    down, setting to rights as might be—
And I am beguiled by her report and letters of honest
    citizens to the paper.
They tell in such trust and confidence.
It was like the deluge on the eve of the Battle of
    Waterloo, one gentleman reports—
With a dragon in the sky!

> A 2x4 scantling hurled through a post oak;
> Dr. Luther Jones's son found with a beam in his forehead;
> The Widow Foles and her five children killed outright
>   and buried in one grave;
> John Crawford's family drowned in a cellar;
> Mrs. Collins's infant snatched from her arms and not
>   found till late Tuesday evening;
> Dried cowhides picked up in Smith County;
> The miraculous life of a dog.

But more than this—much more.
These things were but strange workings, the solace of
    life when you come to think of it—mischievous imps
    on a cathedral frieze.
Good people looked up and smiled,
Forging anew their one great pronouncement.

Rube Burrows On The Buckatunna Trestle, Looking North

They cased the town on Sunday—Rube, Joe, and
    Rube Smith, that greenhorn boy.
Rube Burrows never said a word.
Wednesday was the day though.
They cooked on the fireplace, ate, slept, and
    looked at one another.
On Wednesday evening, Rube went back alone.
Standing on the trestle, looking north, he might
    have been in church,
One of the Elect!
It's the knowing that matters.
He liked to say they didn't know Rube Burrows, but
    that they'd find out.
And they did—
At half past two in the morning, when No. 10 pulled
    up to the water tank on time.
But not to take on water.

Rube got better and better. He took out his last
    train alone—he didn't need anybody.
When they killed him, his father brought him home
    from Sulligent in the wagon.
They sang "Rock of Ages" at Fellowship Baptist
    Church and covered his grave with fall flowers.

The Land Office In Holly Springs

When the Indians gave up their land in the
    thirties,
Government built this house on Gholson to sell
    deeds in.
After the war, Mr. James Holland made a pretty
    place of it—he was a bachelor and liked to
    have his friends in;
And when trouble came again to the country in
    '78—Grenada in panic! People fleeing,
    their arms to Heaven!—
Mr. Holland said, Come! Come stay with me!
And met two guests at the train.
He put Mr. Downs in the back room,
Because Miss Lake— if she might—preferred
    the front parlor.
One week later, on Saturday night, Mr. Downs
    skipped out.
Out the back window, without notice!—
So as not to disturb Miss Lake, who was unwell.
The next morning when church bells rang,
    just across the street,
A few gathered but didn't go in—
Their eyes on the little frame house!
The Land Office, they called it—
Where a different warrant was issued in the old
    days,
And gigs whipped off to grand estate.

Ubi Sunt

When the crop-duster dives in the Delta—
    no cover to run to!
And I remember in Faulkner cypress and gum,
      pinoak and ash, and a tree full of squirrels
      in a clearing.
Now there is only a pecan orchard, with a
    sign out.
I feel the same way around Hattiesburg—
And once foolishly asked a professor if there
      wasn't somewhere a little woods left;
An acre or two, just for the feeling—
One tree, please, to take a bearing from?
And I remember a creek bottom at home before the
      expressway came through,
Where a cornfield was and a truckpatch.
But to what purpose?
What can anyone do—
What could even Faulkner do, except to put forward
      that these things once were?

I Think His Folks Started The Town

Rock Chapel is worth seeing.
Just a little beyond Pope—you see it before
     you get there,
Across from the Rock Store.

> "Pope Chapel AME Zion Church was
> built with the design of Bishop B .G.
> Shaw, a united community & the skill
> of one man, Rev. C. B. Simmons from Tn."

It was 8:00 in the morning with a cloud coming
     up,
When William Pope pulled in with his good manners
     and brightened the day.
He showed us the upstairs and downstairs, proud
     to tell about it. They brought the rock over
     from Sardis Dam, before he was born, because
     nobody else wanted it.
They brought it in with wagon and mules, some-
     times after dark, and put it up with their hands.
A fine undertaking, for all men to see.
And when the wind and rain came that morning,
It felt good to be with William in a firm-foundation
     church.

On the way back to old 51,
Crossing the tracks by the ghost stores where the
     white people live,
Surely, I said, there are many little towns like
     Pope that have seen better days—

                                        And

And men of Bethel, building for their children—
Getting on with it together, but taking time out
    for the stranger.
I didn't ask William, but like to think his folks
    started the town.
He seemed to belong there.

If You Go To Cascilla In The Summertime

On my way to Cascilla last summer—from
    the west, up Valley Road—
I pulled off to see—what I knew I didn't
    want to see:
A craze on the land—the Delta bluffs under
    sorcery!
Easter Island.
Great plinths rose out of the depths, satin-
    draped in the sun—
And every green god clung to a shell!
I cannot admire predatory beauty—it's not
    right in our country!
Where did it come from—and who's going to
    answer for it?
For something's on the move, crawling like
    snakes.
One wonders about Cascilla up there.
They say the old post office is already gone.
And what about Jamie Whitten's place?

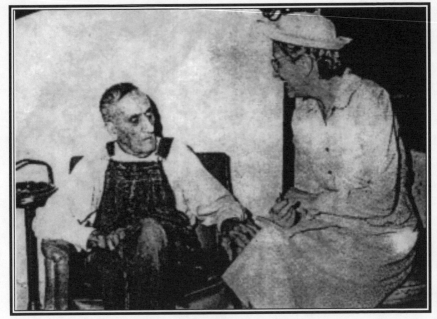

Charlie Walton, age 85, of the Friendship Community, giving Zereda Greene information about the last ferry boat, and the ferryman, Mr. Billy Walton, his great-uncle. He helped build the last ferry.

Photo by Jimmy Comer

Miss Zereda

Wherever mailboxes stood, old people waited on
    Thursday morning,
Turning to obituaries first, then to Miss Zereda.
She had a hat shop just off the square and wore a
    little hat over the counter.
That was the sounding post, picking up things while
    she did the talking.
It happened before our time, before streets were paved
    and electric lights got out of town.
Her people came from over at Mooreville and the
    Carolina-Bigby Fork community, half a day's trip
    either way.
But a wagon ride in summer was life: all-day singings,
    protracted meetings, picnics and candidate-speakings
    around the Fourth.
Memory was history—watching Halley's Comet with two
    old slaves (who remembered from the other time); the
    last ride on the ferry before the Bankhead came
    through; Court Week, which was like a fair;
    children playing in the old jail, the rape of
    the old courthouse.
The town changed, but Miss Zereda didn't change.
She wore her hat, stuck to facts, and prevailed for
    Itawamba County—
A little speck of life thrown off from the mass, burning
    out alone.

Even young people looked up.
They read "These Things I Remember," smiled and shook
    their heads—
And were satisfied with their lives.

The Tree That Went To The Moon

When I asked about the tree that went to
    the moon,
The young lady waited for me to say something
    else.
She looked at her neighbor, chuckled—but got
    on the telephone.
I was in and out of Dorman Hall everywhere that
    morning, like a round robin—
And people noticed.
Once I broke off for another run out to the tree.
Then, somebody said Dr. Mullenax would know if
    anybody did.
I liked Dr. Mullenax's secretary.
She put her boss to work and asked me to take a
    chair.
"I wouldn't know a sycamore if I saw one," she
    said—and I went out to get her a leaf, which
    she thanked me for and laid beside her computer.
Dr. Mullenax had got as far as the Vice-President,
    she said. I hoped I wouldn't have to see him.
Then Dr. Mullenax came in, looking pleased.
"Where IS this tree?" he said.
On the way out I told him about another tree I found last
    week—but I think one was enough for the
    morning.
It's only a sycamore of course, like any
    on a creekbank—
But seems already to have taken on presence.
We looked at it.
It knows who it is.

Governor Bilbo's Screen Porch

Governor Bilbo stood up for the common man.
He cut taxes, built roads and hospitals, dug
     dipping vats for constituent cows, and
     delivered free textbooks to schoolchildren.
He also came out for clean government.
But every time I walk down Capitol Street—to
     lunch in the Elite Cafe—
I celebrate one thing he didn't do.
He didn't like the big house he lived in—
     "the handsomest abode in the Southern county,"
     DeBow's Review called it in 1842—
And tried to sell it off.
"Tear down this relic of royalty!" he said.
Not succeeding, however—the ladies caught him
     with his shirttail out—
He settled for a screen porch! And slept
     on the porte-cochère!
Which they took out later of course.
So, the next time you walk down Capitol Street,
     have another look:

> The Grecian portico, semicircular
> and elegant, relieving the severity
> of the box-like design...

Tuesday

~~Saturday,~~ January 25, 1910

"Lest We Forget." My birthday!
Forty-Two years old today.
I can scarcely realize it
yet when I stop to think,
many eventful years have
passed over my head, nine-
teen glad happy years with
out a care; Then loss of
loved ones - my first marriage, the loss of my dear
Mother, my husband's death
a few years later, my Auntie's
death nine years ago (1900, July 4)
my second marriage to Mr. Bu-
el Sept 12, 1905 and my dear
Father's death Nov 3, 1907. He
lived to see my husband elected
Governor. Much sorrow but
God has been very good. My children spared and in good health.
My husband honored, and I shar-
ing his position. God is truly good to

80

On Finding The Governor Noel Diaries

When I heard that the house in Lexington still
    stands, I bestirred old bones.
The pretty young wife who appeared at the door
    was only a little puzzled—
And such is the efficacy of trust in her country
    that the stranger walked in an honored guest.
She knew nothing though, she said. Nothing—
Pulling off the dog and a baby or two, calling
    to the nurse in the kitchen. Her husband had
    just left for the office.
But had oftened wondered.
And—remembering—there lay behind me on the
    whatnot, if I would be so kind as to reach
    around,
Seven little books! Dainty, done-up—like something
    for the children to play with.
Five were the Governor's, two his lady's.
"May I see!" I said, standing up.
"Of course," she laughed—she just hadn't got
    around to them—and led me to a writing desk by
    the window.
She was off—and forgot all about me.

> Alice T. Noel-
> Governor's Mansion, Jackson, Miss.
>   In this book is recorded some of the
> events occurring during the third year
> of Governor Noel's administration.
>   *January 1, 1910:*
>   *A lovely New Year. The*
>   *Governor's staff called to*
>   *wish us a Happy New Year:*
>   *Colonel Walls, Major Carl*
>   *Decatur, Captain Coffee…*

                And

And so I came up on history.
But what could I do? Unmanned by the manners of
    that house, of which I was a part now and
        disposed of—
And by light in that room!
My mistress came by without glancing—a carpenter was
    at the door for instructions.
It was partly for history that they bought the house,
    she said.
"And we want to know more! As the children grow up."
The past is precious and must be preserved—
And looks very well on the whatnot.

Larry Brown's Coyote Pups

Larry Brown's country around Yocona was once
   a great forest:
Hickory and oak, beech and gum—riddled with
   squirrels' nests.
Now the whole state's a pine tree—and bugs
   are eating it!
This cultivated wildness—an element in his
   fiction I believe—has brought in new
   things,
The coyote, for example.
One day he found a nest of coyote pups in a
   culvert, not a hundred yards from his house.
"I could see them with a flashlight, all eyes,
   faces, and fur, backed up in the darkness."
It took him two days to dig them out;
But out they came—no whine, no snarl: six
   little wild things absolutely still.
But with horrible fangs—to kill and eat dogs!
Wild is a category of its own, Mr. Brown says,
   that tame can never approach—
Which strikes me as something to think about.
What does one do with coyote pups?
(His children admired them, the neighbors came
   in to see.)
The eternal question—
Posed for Larry Brown on the back of his pickup.

M.B.   L.D.

BY M.B. MAYFIELD - '96

Ecru

It was on his line—
Though after Ingomar, Colonel Falkner didn't
    need another town on his railroad.
Still, the little yellow station caught on.
People moved in—and the twins of Ecru
    looked just alike.
But they weren't alike, of course.
One wasn't like anybody!
When they laid him on the pallet, he crawled
    off backwards!
Backing up, backing up—Just look at that
    young'n!—
Till he found a corner and sat, being peaceful
    with himself.
He wove beautiful things with his hands and
    and his heart, holding them out.
His mother stood back and smiled. It wasn't
    long.
He became a man; and with destiny upon him
They heard from far off—and came to Ecru
    bearing gifts;
Or at least with money in their pockets.
Being directed at the post office, north out of
    town up Old 15,
To knock at his door—
And to see!

The Big Woods

"**A** rapturous country!" Claiborne called it,
    after a journey by horseback in 1841.
"I have never seen so happy a people."
It was in fact like an ocean—rolling—in
    unison with deep grasses.
Or like a church.
Then the saws came—
And squirrels on Treetop I-59 had to find
    another way.
They burned Jackson twice one summer—
I'd rather have been there both times than
    to wake every morning to that sound.
The deer heard and looked up; bison and boar, the
    paroquet and pigeon—all things that live with
    leaves.
Of course they heard.
They stilled a moment—and went back to work.
For what is there to do at Armageddon but lift
    your head and keep on awhile?

Honeymoon In Jefferson

The room was like an aerie.
After showing them up, Miss Elma came
    back down and brushed her hands—
But the bronzed young man came back too.
He'd spied a setup in the backyard—and
    took up there, looking out on the old
    Rowland place;
And off and on seemed to be writing a letter.

      "I want some poison," the lady said.
    She looked at the druggist with cold
    haughty eyes, her face like a strained
    flag.
      "Why, of course," the druggist said, *"if that's
    what you want, but the law says…"*
      "I want arsenic," the lady said.

The Devil was in it—laying the pencil down.
    In everything of course. A matter of impure
    properties.
The house he drew in ivy and old rot was con-
    demned by the city. They said it was coming
    down—
There where she stopped them dead in their
    tracks; *"I have no taxes in Jefferson."*

Meanwhile, in valanced dark—quite unprepared
    for this!—
A little hand waited on the mantelpiece.
Old brides waited too, craned at windows, caging
    the afternoon—
While the young man in shirtsleeves wrote on,
    indifferent, virginal.
Neat as art.

They Also Set Out Kudzu

The CCC celebrated trees.
A few of their parks are left in the state, and
    my favorite is Tishomingo, in the Tennessee Hills.
The Natchez Trace runs right through it.
Though he never saw it, our great idealist President
    designed Tishomingo, as he did all the parks, in
    a Sherwood Forest mood:
Young men sleeping under trees, going out in the
    morning to set out more trees.
Mr. Royce Buckner, the manager, showed me around.
First, they built—from a quarry on the mountain—
    the manager's house and the cabin I would sleep in;
The Lodge (on the second highest point in the State
    of Mississippi),
And the 99 steps leading down to Bear Creek and the
    Swinging Bridge, which you can still cross over;
Also the spillway by the log cabin.
But the CCC boys' business was trees. They were
    already setting out trees in fact—
All over the country, all over the world!
Long leaf, short leaf, loblolly, slash—not to
    mention the other kind.
A brotherhood of trees!
They also set out kudzu.

IV

Late Thoughts

Horn Island

I like the saga of Walter Anderson and an
    occasional passage in his journals.
His painting I don't understand.
A fierce man—even with creatures he
    loved—he saw too clearly to be a friend.
"Man here is far away," he once wrote on
    arriving at Horn. "How pleasant without
    him."

        Coming back to camp, I thought of
        God and a white Heron flew up; and a
        little later when I thought of man—
        a Red Winged Black Bird flushed. I
        also jumped a bobolink but I think my
        mind was blank at the time. It was
        in full plummage.

I remember the old museum—his little house
    on the Point—with Mary his daughter
    directing a tour through.
His skiff was under the porch, with a reach
    of water below the house.
I don't like to think of those departures—
    nor of the faces who watched from windows.
But I know that he set up some strength on the
    island and went out of himself in strange
    ways. And found joy.
He says so in his journals and I believe also
    in his painting.

The White Pavilion

for Carl Melsone

Miss Welty is not happy with symbols, but
   one I do like.
Leaving her mother and friends at the white
   pavilion one morning,
A young girl went down to the lake to dream.
A party of loud people moved in around her—
   laughing, mocking, ignoring her presence.
   They didn't even see her!
Two boys and a girl kicking sand ran ellipses
   around them;
When the woman raised up from the sand, her
   breasts hung widening, like pears.
("When I was a child, such people were called
   common.")
Then the man saw her. He looked at her and
   smiled, like a dog smiles, panting.
She stilled—the frail stem of neck holding
   at bay;
But didn't stand a chance of course—
Bounding up the green slope in tears, to
   known voices.

When Tennessee Williams Looked Into The Eyes of William Faulkner At A New York Party

With everybody talking at once and moving on
      over to somebody else's place,
He happened to look into the old man's eyes—
      and became very still;
And—so he said—burst into tears.
The two were much alike actually, bred to the
      heart, starting out on that premise.
But something had happened to the distinguished
      guest.
He didn't have anything to say.
He just sat there.
Could it be that he didn't like camp? A matter
      of gravitas—and being so far from home?
Or, just that he didn't know how to do at the
      party,
And they were beginning to look at him.

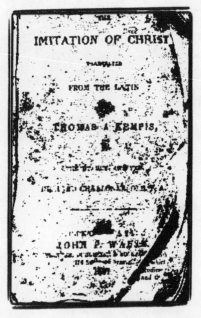

TITLE PAGE OF "THE IMITATION OF CHRIST,"
by Thomas A. Kempis, the little volume used by
Jefferson Davis during his imprisonment at Fortress
Monroe, which contains many notations made by
Mr. Davis at that time.

She Asked Him To Read
The Beatitudes

After Fortress Monroe, President Davis came
    home to no country—
Mrs. Sarah Anne Dorsey took him in at Beauvoir;
    and in the East Cottage, where he stayed,
    they listened together.

> *"It's nice to be whipped, quiet to*
> *be whipped—to be whipped and lie under*
> *a broken roof thinking of home."*

In return, one night while lying in Charity
    Hospital in New Orleans,
She asked him to read the Beatitudes to her—
And in the morning she died.
I don't know why I remember this.
He had Beauvoir now—his family, friends,
    the old associations.
But this was a new possession, a new kind of
    knowledge.
In the long afternoons while writing his history,
    he walked out alone to the orange grove and
    the old vineyard.
Sometimes he stopped off at the little spring.

When I Walked Over Fairfield Farm

What trick of earth is this!
When Governor James Coleman died, they took
    away the dirt from his grave in Ackerman—
    so ordered in his will—
And brought in from where he plowed at Fairfield.
When I walked over Fairfield Farm, I saw what
    he meant—
But could have seen in the meanest plot:
The rabbit returns to his burrow at dark;
The field mouse to his cornstalk;
Bedded down in her stall, the cow has nothing
    to wish for—
So why shouldn't man speak out with a little
    gesture?
Only a big man though could show his heart
    like that.

Oscar Wilde At Beauvoir

Mr. Davis retired early, a matter of health—
Leaving the guest to his wife and to Winnie;
Who, with ever so slight a German charm, had
    nothing to fear from the young man, nothing
    to gain.
Mrs. Davis approved from the start, his spirits,
    style—he was amusing.
As for Mr. Wilde—bearing inexplicably Mr. Davis's
    great tome about the country,
Reposing it would seem on jowled heaviness (with
    a repartee deploying beneath)—
What did he think?
What was he doing there?
Relieved no doubt that the President walked out
(He would certainly leave the photograph now),
He fell into amiability with the house, the ménage,
    and swept Varina out to an old suzerainty—
Smiling on her guests, knowing discreetly, tapping
    a general's arm with her fan.
A masque affair.
A drag.

After adieux, past midnight,
The guest walked out under the oak trees.
Beauty lay on the earth, a thousand flowers, quite
    helpless;
The tide stretched out its hands.
And there was the crux!
A splendor of stars—and Richmond!
To know in the mouth the sad necessity—that's why
    he came to Beauvoir.

On Seeing Sgt. Jake Lindsay's Picture
On The Cover of Life Magazine

He came from a farm south of Lucedale—
And race was in the face—the ancient Highlands
    and hills of home.
It was a quiet face.

> For conspicuous gallantry
> and intrepidity at the risk of
> his own life, above and beyond
> the call of duty...

Four days and four nights, Tech. Sgt. Jake W.
    Lindsay and his six men (forty to begin with)
    held on in the Huertgen Forest.
"I stopped the first tank when it was ten yards
    in front of me. The crew got out and we killed
    them."
When they ran out of ammunition, Sgt. Lindsay
    killed three men with his bayonet.
They killed and killed and didn't surrender.
It's hard to describe how I felt when I read
    that.
Mainly though, as I said, it was the face.
The morning he left home they sat down to breakfast
    by a coal oil lamp.

Stopping Off By A
Confederate Graveyard

It's fine to stand where brave men died,
    fine to submit to their mastery.
But there was only one way for them.
They arose on that morning with certainty and
    a long stride. The rain didn't matter—ten
    thousand foes!
Behind them lay the fair country...
"O alchemist Alighieri!" a great poet cried,
"How distant from your harmony that cosmos in
    which I perish!"
He had intellect and knowledge, the great poet,
    and could make learned allusion;
Reminding me of how little I know.
But we all know, don't we?
These white slabs consigned to order,
And the tattered ranks on scene at sundown—
    with an unexpected line from a poem—
All stand up dumb together.

The Church of Our Saviour

On Finding The Church
Of Our Saviour

Coming down from old Eastport, I saw it—
    board-and-batten beauty set skyward! On
    Eastport Street.
I got out of my car still looking—being
    sorrowful already though, suspecting the
    truth.
They stand in small towns all up and down the
    country, where the old families have died
    out;
For a ghostly service once a year perhaps—
    or commissioned like Our Saviour to more
    immediate purpose:
St. Clement's in Vaiden; Immanuel, Winona; Christ
    Church, Church Hill; St. John's, Glen Allan.
I stood a long time before St. Mary's at
    Enterprise, not wanting to find out—
    and Ascension at Brooksville.
We must be grateful of course for what was.
(Bishop Green's on his way! Somebody saw his
    horse!)
But museums make me sad---and the infinite care
    of the state, in a land of spires with no place
    to kneel.
I took my picture but didn't try to go in.

Voices On Deer Creek

Stopping off on Deer Creek to see Kermit and
    his friends,
I was confused by voices!
They sounded all right on Sesame Street. I
    thought Kermit was from off anyway.
For Deer Creek is an honorable stream, though
    not granted the dignity of river,
And brings beauty to little towns all through
    the Delta.
So I turned from the information desk and a
    machine getting ready to go
For the platform—and a wide soft morning.
The creek was fat, the sun felt good on
    my shoulders.
The fact is, the voices were wrong!—
On the surface, scratching, like an old
    phonograph record.
Let us consider voices—so important in human
    relations.
Once upon a time when creatures talked, an old
    man and a boy sat by the fire:

> "Next day, Mr. Rabbit and Miss Rabbit
> got up early, fo' day, and raided the
> gyarden—like yo' Maw's out dar—and
> got some cabbiges and roas'n years..."

It's not the story that matters, even the boy
    knew that,
But something in the telling, the sound.
("I hear Miss Sally calling, honey. You better
    run along now.")
Not the word but the fall behind it,
The pitch that lingers unfathomed.

Race Relations In Mississippi

When I went in from Pump No. 1—somewhere
    around Grenada—
The young black woman said, Good Morning!—
    while looking down at her feet.
I told you it ain't there! she said to her feet.
A white man with a bald spot raised up to counter
    level and said, Morning!
She got the machine going and without looking
    at anybody said out to the world, It
    ain't there!
I got my change, another smile and Have-a-Nice-
    Day.
Come back, the man said down below.
I hated to leave them like that.
When I looked back at the door, she was down
    there with him.
They still hadn't found it.

ACKNOWLEDGEMENTS

p. 14   "The Burial of DeSoto" is one of five mural paint-
ings by Newton Alonzo Wells executed in the
1890's for the Gayoso Hotel in Memphis. Four can
now be seen in the DeSoto County Courthouse
in Hernando. J. B. Bell, THE HERNANDO
DeSOTO NARRATIVE (Hernando, 1989).
By permission of J. B. Bell.

p. 17   William Faulkner, REQUIEM FOR A NUN
(New York: Random House, 1951).

p. 21   Albert J. Pickett, HISTORY OF ALABAMA,
AND INCIDENTALLY OF GEORGIA AND
MISSISSIPPI (Charleston: Walker & James,
1851). 2 vols.

p. 23   J. F. H. Claiborne, MISSISSIPPI AS A
PROVINCE, TERRITORY AND STATE
(Jackson: Power & Barksdale, 1880).

p. 24   Hinda and Hafed, "Lalla Rookh," POETICAL
WORKS OF THOMAS MOORE (New York:
Robert Martin, 1851).

p. 26   Photo by Norman Ezell.

p. 28   "Governor Mathews," by the late Samuel Vadah
Cochran. By permission of Doris S. Cochran,
Executor.

p. 35   J. F. H. Claiborne, LIFE AND CORRESPON-
DENCE OF JOHN A. QUITMAN (New York:
Harper & Bros., 1860). 2 vols.

p. 42   THE DIARY OF EUGENIA LEVY PHILLIPS,
Phillips & Myers Family Papers in the Southern
Historical Collection, Wilson Library, The
University of North Carolina at Chapel Hill.

p. 49   D. Morris, THE COLONY OF BRITISH
HONDURAS (London: Edward Stanford, 1883).

p. 52   Clifton L. Taulbert, ONCE UPON A TIME
        WHEN WE WERE COLORED (Tulsa: Council
        Oak Books, 1989).

p. 56   Photo by Don G. Sanders.

p. 65   Mary Craig Kimbrough Sinclair, SOUTHERN
        BELLE (New York: Crown Publishers, 1957). By
        permission of David Sinclair.

p. 68   Louise Anderson, THE CEMETERIES OF
        JEFFERSON DAVIS COUNTY (North Little
        Rock: 1989).

p. 76   ITAWAMBA COUNTY TIMES, July 29, 1965.

p. 80   THE DIARY OF ALICE T. NOEL. By permission
        of Mr. and Mrs. Pat Barrett, Jr.

p. 84   "The Baby Who Crawled SDRAWKCAB"
        by M. B. Mayfield. By permission of M.B. Mayfield.

p. 91   THE HORN ISLAND LOGS OF WALTER
        INGLIS ANDERSON, ed. Redding S. Sugg, Jr.
        (Jackson: University Press of Missisipi, 1985).

p. 94   Dunbar Rowland, HISTORY OF MISSISSIPPI:
        HEART OF THE SOUTH (Chicago: S. J. Clarke
        Publishing Co., 1925). 4 vols.

Designed, Produced, and Distributed by
Langford & Associates
3307 Park Avenue
Memphis, Tennessee 38111
(901) 324-8769   FAX (901) 458-4151

Typography by
The Composing Room, Inc.
3314 Park Avenue
Memphis, Tennessee 38111

9.2.06